This book belongs to:

....

....

For Matthew, my adventurous little boy, who inspired this story!
Lots of love from Mummy xxx

Editors: Tasha Percy and Sophie Hallam
Designer: Anna Lubecka
Editorial Director: Victoria Garrard
Art Director: Laura Roberts-Jensen

Copyright © QED Publishing 2015

First published in the UK in 2015 by QED Publishing
Part of The Quarto Group, The Old Brewery, 6 Blundell Street, London, N7 9BH

www.qed-publishing.co.uk

A catalogue record for this book is available from the British Library.

ISBN 978 1 78493 243 5

Printed in China

Be Careful, Barney!

Written and illustrated by Lucy Barnard

Barney was a very adventurous little fox cub.
His mummy would always shout,

"Be careful, Barney!"

But he just
wouldn't listen.

At the park, Barney would always choose the **biggest** slide.

Then he'd **swing** really **high**, and leap off mid-flight.

And he'd hang **upside down** from the climbing frame using just his tail!

He would yell,

"*FASTER!*"

when he was on the
roundabout, even though
his friends wanted to stop.

When Barney's favourite dinosaur toy was put on the top of his shelves, he decided to try and reach it all by himself.

Oh dear!

Barney also loved to dress up as
a superhero and would pretend
to fly by jumping off his cupboard.

"Wheeeee!"

One day, Barney's class
went on a school trip.

At lunchtime, they stopped for a picnic.
Mrs Badger told the class not to go near the
river but Barney wanted to have some fun.

He was balancing on the first stepping stone when...

"Barney, come away
from the river!"

Mrs Badger's
booming
voice startled
poor Barney
and he began to
wobble.

With his paws

circling wildly

he tried to keep
his balance but it
was too late...

The choppy water swirled around Barney
and carried him quickly down the river.

The rest of the class ran along the riverbank.
Mrs Badger searched frantically
for a way to help Barney.

Suddenly, Barney heard
a roaring, crashing
sound. It was getting
louder and **louder.**

He was being
swept straight
towards a
waterfa**ll!**

"Barney, grab hold of this!"

Trevor said, holding out a long, leafy branch.

Barney managed to grab hold of it just in time.

Mrs Badger and the rest of the class pulled the very wet little fox cub back onto dry land.

Phew!

At hometime, Mrs Badger told Barney's
mummy what had happened.

"Oh Barney," said Mummy, giving him a big hug.
"Do you promise to be more careful?"

"Yes, Mummy,"
promised Barney.

The next day at the park, Barney was high up on the climbing frame and about to jump off...

...when he remembered how worried Mummy had been. He remembered the promise he had made.

So he carefully climbed down and went to find his friends instead. He had just as much fun!

Next steps

Look at the front and back cover of the book together - can the children talk about the differences between Barney and his friends?

When you have read the story together, talk to the children about the things Barney did at the park that were a bit too adventurous. How could he have had fun more safely? Ask them what sorts of things they like to do at the park.

In the story, Barney loves to dress up as a superhero. Ask the children what their favourite dressing-up clothes are.

Barney climbs up his shelves to try and reach his toy dinosaur. Why was this dangerous? What toys do the children have at home that they like to play with?

Why do the children think Barney's mummy always tells him to be careful? Do they think that some of the things that Barney did were a bit silly? What do their parents tell them to do and not to do?

When Barney fell into the river and nearly got swept over the waterfall, his friends were there to help him. Talk to the children about when they have helped or been kind to a friend.

At the end of the story, Barney has learnt his lesson and decides to play with his friends. What sort of games do the children like to play?